KINGFISHER
An imprint of Kingfisher Publications Plc
New Penderel House, 283–288 High Holborn
London WC1V 7HZ
www.kingfisherpub.com

First published in Sweden by Alfabeta Bokförlag
First published in the UK by Kingfisher 2005
1 3 5 7 9 10 8 6 4 2

Text and illustrations copyright © Lars Klinting 1996

A CIP catalogue record for this book is available from the British Library.

ISBN-10: 0 7534 1176 8
ISBN-13: 978 0 7534 1176 6

Printed in Taiwan
1TR/0205/SHENS/SGCH/158MA/F

Harvey the Baker

Lars Klinting

KINGFISHER

Knock! Knock!

Who is knocking on Harvey's window so early in the morning?

It's his friend, Chip. He's come to say
Happy Birthday to Harvey!

Suddenly, Harvey realizes that there's nothing
in the house for Chip to eat.

Of course! He'll bake a birthday cake!
What a great idea.

Harvey's kitchen
has plenty of bowls,
pans and spoons. But he
is missing something important.

Here it is! Chip has found Harvey's cookbook.
It has a recipe for the yummiest birthday cake ever.

Before they start, Harvey reads the recipe carefully.
Then they check to see if they have all the ingredients.

First, Harvey melts some butter in a saucepan. Then he gets ...

some breadcrumbs

a pastry brush

and a cake tin.

Harvey brushes the inside of the cake tin with a little melted butter. While Harvey turns the oven on, Chip pours some breadcrumbs into the cake tin. Then he shakes the tin all about, so the crumbs stick to the butter.

Next, Harvey takes out . . .

sugar

eggs

and his
favourite
bowl. (It's a
bit chipped,
but it's nice
and big!)

Harvey cracks the two eggs open and puts them in the bowl. Chip adds the sugar.

Then Harvey takes out his electric mixer. It can mix things together very quickly.

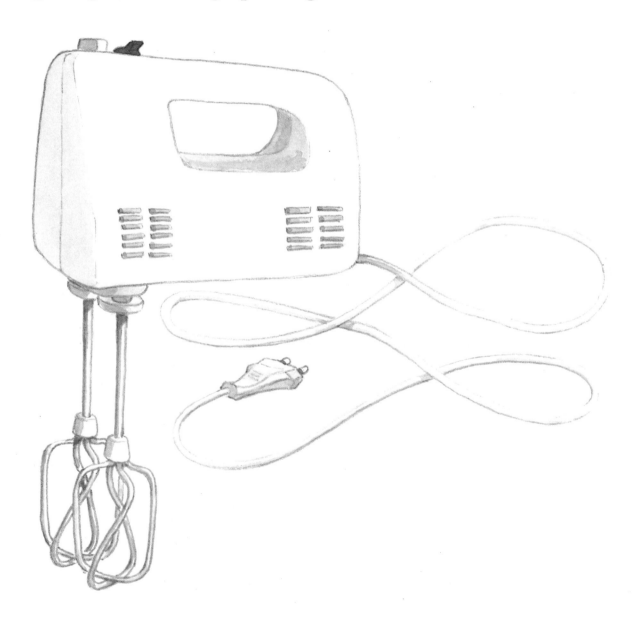

Harvey beats the eggs and sugar together until they are fluffy. What a lot of noise the mixer makes!

Now Harvey puts . . .

baking powder

vanilla extract

and flour in a
small bowl and
mixes them
together.

Chip takes
out a wooden spoon . . .

and milk.

It's time to pour the milk and melted butter into the mixture. Then Chip adds the flour, vanilla and baking powder from the small bowl. Harvey stirs it all together. The kitchen is starting to get a bit messy!

Chip helps Harvey pour the cake mixture into the baking tin.

Some of the cake mixture sticks to the bowl,
so Chip licks it up – yummy!

Now the cake is ready to go in the oven.
Watch out, Chip – it's hot!

The oven has a glass window, so Harvey and Chip can watch their cake rise as it bakes. It's almost as much fun as watching TV! Harvey sets the timer, so they will know when the cake is ready.

Just look at the mess they've made!
They'd better get that cleaned up.

While the cake is baking, there's time to do the dishes. Harvey washes and Chip dries, so it doesn't take long at all.

The cake is ready, but they need to let it cool off a bit before they can eat it. It smells wonderful! Chip can hardly wait to taste it.

Chip puts a doily on
top of the cake.

Then he puts a plate
upside down on top.

Harvey turns the cake
out of the baking tin.

Ta da!

Doesn't it look lovely?

Harvey and Chip take out . . .

a tablecloth

glasses

juice

napkins

plates

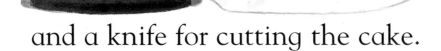
and a knife for cutting the cake.

They set the table and sit down. But just as they're about to cut the cake, the doorbell rings.

Quick, Chip! Set out some more plates.

Happy Birthday to you.
Happy Birthday to you.
Happy Birthday, dear Harvey.
Happy Birthday to you!

It's lucky they made a cake!
There's plenty to go round.

Harvey's Cake

With a grown-up's help, you can make
a cake just like Harvey and Chip!

100 g butter
100 g sugar
2 eggs
100 g plain flour
2 teaspoons baking powder
2 teaspoons vanilla extract
50 ml milk
breadcrumbs

1) Pre-heat the oven to 180º C.

2) Melt the butter in a saucepan over low heat.

3) With a pastry brush, brush the baking tin with a little melted butter.

4) Pour a handful of breadcrumbs into the baking tin and shake carefully, so the breadcrumbs stick to the tin.

5) Beat the eggs and sugar together until fluffy.

6) Mix together flour, baking powder and vanilla extract in a small bowl.

7) Add flour mixture to the eggs and sugar.

8) Add the melted butter and milk to the mixture.

9) Pour the mixture into the cake tin.

10) Bake the cake for approximately 35 minutes, until risen and golden.

The
End